# Gaspar Ruiz

Joseph Conrad

# Table of Contents

# Gaspar Ruiz

## Joseph Conrad

# I

A REVOLUTIONARY war raises many strange characters out of the obscurity which is the common lot of humble lives in an undisturbed state of society.

Certain individualities grow into fame through their vices and their virtues, or simply by their actions, which may have a temporary importance; and then they become forgotten. The names of a few leaders alone survive the end of armed strife and are further preserved in history; so that, vanishing from men's active memories, they still exist in books.

# Gaspar Ruiz

The name of General Santierra attained that cold, paper–and–ink immortality. He was a South American of good family, and the books published in his lifetime numbered him amongst the liberators of that continent from the oppressive rule of Spain.

That long contest, waged for independence on one side and for dominion on the other, developed, in the course of years and the vicissitudes of changing fortune, the fierceness and inhumanity of a struggle for life. All feelings of pity and compassion disappeared in the growth of political hatred. And, as is usual in war, the mass of the people, who had the least to gain by the issue, suffered most in their obscure persons and their humble fortunes.

General Santierra began his service as lieutenant in the patriot army raised and commanded by the famous San Martin, afterwards conqueror of Lima and liberator of Peru. A great battle had just been fought on the banks of the river Bio–Bio. Amongst the prisoners made upon the routed Royalist troops there was a soldier called Gaspar Ruiz. His powerful build and his big head rendered him remarkable amongst his fellow–captives. The personality of the man was unmistakable. Some months before, he had been missed from the ranks of Republican troops after one of the many skirmishes which preceded the great battle. And now, having been captured arms in hand amongst Royalists, he could expect no other fate but to be shot as a deserter.

Gaspar Ruiz, however, was not a deserter; his mind was hardly active enough to take a discriminating view of the advantages or perils of treachery. Why should he change sides? He had really been made a prisoner, had suffered ill–usage and many privations. Neither side showed tenderness to its adversaries. There came a day when he was ordered, together with some other captured rebels, to march in the front rank of the Royal troops. A musket, had been thrust into his hands. He had taken it. He had marched. He did not want to be killed with circumstances of peculiar atrocity for refusing to march. He did not understand heroism, but it was his intention to throw his musket away at the first opportunity. Meantime he had gone on loading and firing, from fear of having his brains blown out, at the first sign of unwillingness, by some non–commissioned officer of the King of Spain. He tried to set forth these elementary considerations before the sergeant of the guard set over him and some twenty other such deserters, who had been condemned summarily to be shot.

# Gaspar Ruiz

It was in the quadrangle of the fort at the back of the batteries which command the road—stead of Valparaiso. The officer who had identified him had gone on without listening to his protestations. His doom was sealed; his hands were tied very tightly together behind his back; his body was sore all over from the many blows with sticks and butts of muskets which had hurried him along on the painful road from the place of his capture to the gate of the fort. This was the only kind of systematic attention the prisoners had received from their escort during a four days' journey across a scantily watered tract of country. At the crossings of rare streams they were permitted to quench their thirst by lapping hurriedly like dogs. In the evening a few scraps of meat were thrown amongst them as they dropped down dead— beat upon the stony ground of the halting—place.

As he stood in the courtyard of the castle in the early morning, after having been driven hard all night, Gaspar Ruiz's throat was parched, and his tongue felt very large and dry in his mouth.

And Gaspar Ruiz, besides being very thirsty, was stirred by a feeling of sluggish anger, which he could not very well express, as though the vigour of his spirit were by no means equal to the strength of his body.

The other prisoners in the batch of the condemned hung their heads, looking obstinately on the ground. But Gaspar Ruiz kept on repeating: "What should I desert for to the Royalists? Why should I desert? Tell me, Estaban!"

He addressed himself to the sergeant, who happened to belong to the same part of the country as himself. But the sergeant, after shrugging his meagre shoulders once, paid no further attention to the deep murmuring voice at his back. It was indeed strange that Gaspar Ruiz should desert. His people were in too humble a station to feel much the disadvantages of any form of government. There was no reason why Gaspar Ruiz should wish to uphold in his own person the rule of the King of Spain. Neither had he been anxious to exert himself for its subversion. He had joined the side of Independence in an extremely reasonable and natural manner. A band of patriots appeared one morning early, surrounding his father's ranche, spearing the watch—dogs and hamstringing a fat cow all in the twinkling of an eye, to the cries of "Viva La Libertad!" Their officer discoursed of Liberty with enthusiasm and eloquence after a long and refreshing sleep. When they left in the evening, taking with them some of Ruiz, the father's, best horses to replace their own lamed animals, Gaspar Ruiz went away with them, having been invited pressingly to do so by the eloquent officer.

Shortly afterwards a detachment of Royalist troops, coming to pacify the district, burnt the ranche, carried off the remaining horses and cattle, and having thus deprived the old people of all their worldly possessions, left them sitting under a bush in the enjoyment of the inestimable boon of life.

## II

GASPAR Ruiz, condemned to death as a deserter, was not thinking either of his native place or of his parents, to whom he had been a good son on account of the mildness of his character and the great strength of his limbs. The practical advantage of this last was made still more valuable to his father by his obedient disposition. Gaspar Ruiz had an acquiescent soul.

But it was stirred now to a sort of dim revolt by his dislike to die the death of a traitor. He was not a traitor. He said again to the sergeant: "You know I did not desert, Estaban. You know I remained behind amongst the trees with three others to keep the enemy back while the detachment was running away!"

Lieutenant Santierra, little more than a boy at the time, and unused as yet to the sanguinary imbecilities of a state of war, had lingered near by, as if fascinated by the sight of these men who were to be shot presently—"for an example"—as the Commandante had said.

The sergeant, without deigning to look at the prisoner, addressed himself to the young officer with a superior smile.

"Ten men would not have been enough to make him a prisoner, mi teniente. Moreover, the other three rejoined the detachment after dark. Why should he, unwounded and the strongest of them all, have failed to do so?"

"My strength is as nothing against a mounted man with a lasso," Gaspar Ruiz protested eagerly. "He dragged me behind his horse for half a mile."

# Gaspar Ruiz

At this excellent reason the sergeant only laughed contemptuously. The young officer hurried away after the Commandante.

Presently the adjutant of the castle came by. He was a truculent, raw– boned man in a ragged uniform. His spluttering voice issued out of a flat, yellow face. The sergeant learned from him that the condemned men would not be shot till sunset. He begged then to know what he was to do with them meantime.

The adjutant looked savagely round the courtyard, and, pointing to the door of a small dungeon–like guard–room, receiving light and air through one heavily–barred window, said: "Drive the scoundrels in there."

The sergeant, tightening his grip upon the stick he carried in virtue of his rank, executed this order with alacrity and zeal. He hit Gaspar Ruiz, whose movements were slow, over his head and shoulders. Gaspar Ruiz stood still for a moment under the shower of blows, biting his lip thoughtfully as if absorbed by a perplexing mental process—then followed the others without haste. The door was locked, and the adjutant carried off the key.

By noon the heat of that low vaulted place crammed to suffocation had become unbearable. The prisoners crowded towards the window, begging their guards for a drop of water; but the soldiers remained lying in indolent attitudes wherever there was a little shade under a wall, while the sentry sat with his back against the door smoking a cigarette, and raising his eyebrows philosophically from time to time. Gaspar Ruiz had pushed his way to the window with irresistible force. His capacious chest needed more air than the others; his big face, resting with its chin on the ledge, pressed close to the bars, seemed to support the other faces crowding up for breath. From moaned entreaties they had passed to desperate cries, and the tumultuous howling of those thirsty men obliged a young officer who was just then crossing the courtyard to shout in order to make himself heard.

"Why don't you give some water to these prisoners!"

The sergeant, with an air of surprised innocence, excused himself by the remark that all those men were condemned to die in a very few hours.

# Gaspar Ruiz

Lieutenant Santierra stamped his foot. "They are condemned to death, not to torture," he shouted. "Give them some water at once."

Impressed by this appearance of anger, the soldiers bestirred themselves, and the sentry, snatching up his musket, stood to attention.

But when a couple of buckets were found and filled from the well, it was discovered that they could not be passed through the bars, which were set too close. At the prospect of quenching their thirst, the shrieks of those trampled down in the struggle to get near the opening became very heartrending. But when the soldiers who had lifted the buckets towards the window put them to the ground again helplessly, the yell of disappointment was still more terrible.

The soldiers of the army of Independence were not equipped with canteens. A small tin cup was found, but its approach to the opening caused such a commotion, such yells of rage and' pain in the vague mass of limbs behind the straining faces at the window, that Lieutenant Santierra cried out hurriedly, "No, no—you must open the door, sergeant."

The sergeant, shrugging his shoulders, explained that he had no right to open the door even if he had had the key. But he had not the key. The adjutant of the garrison kept the key. Those men were giving much unnecessary trouble, since they had to die at sunset in any case. Why they had not been shot at once early in the morning he could not understand.

Lieutenant Santierra kept his back studiously to the window. It was at his earnest solicitations that the Commandante had delayed the execution. This favour had been granted to him in consideration of his distinguished family and of his father's high position amongst the chiefs of the Republican party. Lieutenant Santierra believed that the General commanding would visit the fort some time in the afternoon, and he ingenuously hoped that his naive intercession would induce that severe man to pardon some, at least, of those criminals. In the revulsion of his feeling his interference stood revealed now as guilty and futile meddling. It appeared to him obvious that the general would never even consent to listen to his petition. He could never save those men, and he had only made himself responsible for the sufferings added to the cruelty of their fate.

"Then go at once and get the key from the adjutant," said Lieutenant Santierra.

# Gaspar Ruiz

The sergeant shook his head with a sort of bashful smile, while his eyes glanced sideways at Gaspar Ruiz's face, motionless and silent, staring through the bars at the bottom of a heap of other haggard, distorted, yelling faces.

His worship the adjutant de Plaza, the sergeant murmured, was having his siesta; and supposing that he, the sergeant, would be allowed access to him, the only result he expected would be to have his soul flogged out of his body for presuming to disturb his worship's repose. He made a deprecatory movement with his hands, and stood stock–still, looking down modestly upon his brown toes.

Lieutenant Santierra glared with indignation, but hesitated. His handsome oval face, as smooth as a girl's, flushed with the shame of his perplexity. Its nature humiliated his spirit. His hairless upper lip trembled; he seemed on the point of either bursting into a fit of rage or into tears of dismay.

Fifty years later, General Santierra, the venerable relic of revolutionary times, was well able to remember the feelings of the young lieutenant. Since he had given up riding altogether, and found it difficult to walk beyond the limits of his garden, the general's greatest delight, was to entertain in his house the officers of the foreign men–of–war visiting the harbour. For Englishmen he had a preference, as for old companions in arms. English naval men of all ranks accepted his hospitality with curiosity, because he had known Lord Cochrane and had taken part, on board the patriot squadron commanded by that marvellous seaman, in the cutting–out and blockading operations before Callao—an episode of unalloyed glory in the wars of Independence and of endless honour in the fighting tradition of Englishmen. He was a fair linguist, this ancient survivor of the Liberating armies. A trick of smoothing his long white beard whenever he was short of a word in French or English imparted an air of leisurely dignity to the tone of his reminiscences.

# III

"YES, my friends," he used to say to his guests, "what would you have? A youth of seventeen summers, without worldly experience, and owing my rank only to the glorious patriotism of my father, may God rest his soul, I suffered immense humiliation, not so much from the disobedience of That subordinate, who, after all, was responsible for those prisoners; but I suffered because, like the boy I was, I myself dreaded going to the adjutant for the key. I had felt, before, his rough and cutting tongue. Being quite a common fellow, with no merit except his savage valour, he made me feel his contempt and dislike from the first day I joined my battalion in garrison at the fort. It was only a fortnight before! I would have confronted him sword in hand, but I shrank from the mocking brutality of his sneers.

"I don't remember having been so miserable in my life before or since. The torment of my sensibility was so great that I wished the sergeant to fall dead at my feet, and the stupid soldiers who stared at me to turn into corpses; and even those wretches for whom my entreaties had procured a reprieve I wished dead also, because I could not face them without shame. A mephitic heat like a whiff of air from hell came out of that dark place in which they were confined. Those at the window who heard what was going on jeered at me in very desperation; one of these fellows, gone mad no doubt, kept on urging me volubly to order the soldiers to fire through the window. His insane loquacity made my heart turn faint. And my feet were like lead. There was no higher officer to whom I could appeal. I had not even the firmness of spirit to simply go away.

"Benumbed by my remorse, I stood with my back to the window. You must not suppose that all this lasted a long time. How long could it have been? A minute? If you measured by mental suffering it was like a hundred years; a longer time than all my life has been since. No, certainly, it was not so much as a minute. The hoarse screaming of those miserable wretches died out in their dry throats, and then suddenly a voice spoke, a deep voice muttering calmly. It called upon me to turn round.

"That voice, senores, proceeded from the head of Gaspar Ruiz. Of his body I could see nothing. Some of his fellow–captives had clambered upon his back. He was holding them up. His eyes blinked without looking at me. That and the moving of his lips was all he seemed able to manage in his overloaded state. And when I turned round, this head, that seemed more than human size resting on its chin under a multitude of other heads, asked me whether I really desired to quench the thirst of the captives.

"I said, 'Yes, yes!' eagerly, and came up quite close to the window. I was like a child, and did not know what would happen. I was anxious to be comforted in my helplessness and remorse.

# Gaspar Ruiz

"'Have you the authority, senor teniente, to release my wrists from their bonds?' Gaspar Ruiz's head asked me.

"His features expressed no anxiety, no hope; his heavy eyelids blinked upon his eyes that looked past me straight into the courtyard.

"As if in an ugly dream, I spoke, stammering: 'What do you mean? And how can I reach the bonds on your wrists?'

"'I will try what I can do,' he said; and then that large staring head moved at last, and all the wild faces piled up in that window disappeared, tumbling down. He had shaken his load off with one movement, so strong he was.

"And he had not only shaken it off, but he got free of the crush and vanished from my sight. For a moment there was no one at all to be seen at the window. He had swung about, butting and shouldering, clearing a space for himself in the only way he could do it with his hands tied behind his back.

"Finally, backing to the opening, he pushed out to me between the bars his wrists, lashed with many turns of rope. His hands, very swollen, with knotted veins, looked enormous and unwieldy. I saw his bent back. It was very broad. His voice was like the muttering of a bull.

"Cut, senor teniente! Cut!'

"I drew my sword, my new unblunted sword that had seen no service as yet, and severed the many turns of the hide rope. I did this without knowing the why and the wherefore of my action, but as it were compelled by my faith in that man. The sergeant made as if to cry out, but astonishment deprived him of his voice, and he remained standing with his mouth open as if overtaken by sudden imbecility.

"I sheathed my sword and faced the soldiers. An air of awestruck expectation had replaced their usual listless apathy. I heard the voice of Gaspar Ruiz shouting inside, but the words I could not make out plainly. I suppose that to see him with his arms free augmented the influence of his strength: I mean by this, the spiritual influence that with ignorant people attaches to an exceptional degree of bodily vigour. In fact, he was no more to be feared than before, on account of the numbness of his arms and hands, which lasted for some time.

"The sergeant had recovered his power of speech. 'By all the saints!' he cried, 'we shall have to get a cavalry man with a lasso to secure him again, if he is to be led to the place of execution. Nothing less than a good enlazador on a good horse can subdue him. Your worship was pleased to perform a very mad thing.'

"I had nothing to say. I was surprised myself, and I felt a childish curiosity to see what would happen. But the sergeant was thinking of the difficulty of controlling Gaspar Ruiz when the time for making an example would come.

"'Or perhaps,' the sergeant pursued vexedly, 'we shall be obliged to shoot him down as he dashes out when the door is opened.' He was going to give further vent to his anxieties as to the proper carrying out of the sentence; but he interrupted himself with a sudden exclamation, snatched a musket from a soldier, and stood watchful with his eyes fixed on the window.'"

# IV

"GASPAR RUIZ had clambered up on the sill, and sat down there with his feet against the thickness of the wall and his knees slightly bent. The window was not quite broad enough for the length of his legs. It appeared to my crestfallen perception that he meant to keep the window all to himself. He seemed to be taking up a comfortable position. Nobody inside dared to approach him now he could strike with his hands.

"'Por Dios!' I heard the sergeant muttering at my elbow, 'I shall shoot him through the head now, and get rid of that trouble. He is a condemned man.'

"At that I looked at him angrily. 'The general has not confirmed the sentence,' I said—though I knew well in my heart that these were but vain words. The sentence required no confirmation. 'You have no right to shoot him unless he tries to escape,' I added firmly.

"'But sangre de Dios!' the sergeant yelled out, bringing his musket up to the shoulder, 'he is escaping now. Look!'

"But I, as if that Gaspar Ruiz had cast a spell upon me, struck the musket upward, and the bullet flew over the roofs somewhere. The sergeant dashed his arm to the ground and stared. He might have commanded the soldiers to fire, but he did not. And if he had he would not have been obeyed, I think, just then.

"With his feet against the thickness of the wall, and his hairy hands grasping the iron bar, Gaspar sat still. It was an attitude. Nothing happened for a time. And suddenly it dawned upon us that he was straightening his bowed back and contracting his arms. His lips were twisted into a snarl. Next thing we perceived was that the bar of forged iron was being bent slowly by the mightiness of his pull. The sun was beating full upon his cramped, unquivering figure. A shower of sweat–drops burst out of his forehead. Watching the bar grow crooked, I saw a little blood ooze from under his finger–nails. Then he let go. For a moment he remained all huddled up, with a hanging head, looking drowsily into the upturned palms of his mighty hands. Indeed he seemed to have dozed off. Suddenly he flung himself backwards on the sill, and setting the soles of his bare feet against the other middle bar, he bent that one too, but in the opposite direction from the first.

"Such was his strength, which in this case relieved my painful feelings. And the man seemed to have done nothing. Except for the change of position in order to use his feet, which made us all start by its swiftness, my recollection is that of immobility. But he had bent the bars wide apart. And now he could get out if he liked; but he dropped his legs inwards; and looking over his shoulder beckoned to the soldiers. 'Hand up the water,' he said. 'I will give them all a drink.'

"He was obeyed. For a moment I expected man and bucket to disappear, overwhelmed by the rush of eagerness; I thought they would pull him down with their teeth. There was a rush, but holding the bucket on his lap he repulsed the assault of those wretches by the mere swinging of his feet. They flew backwards at every kick, yelling with pain; and the soldiers laughed, gazing at the window.

"They all laughed, holding their sides, except the sergeant, who was gloomy and morose. He was afraid the prisoners would rise and break out—which would have been a bad example. But there was no fear of that, and I stood myself before the window with my drawn sword. When sufficiently tamed by the strength of Gaspar Ruiz, they came up one by one, stretching their necks and presenting their lips to the edge of the bucket which the strong man tilted towards them from his knees with an extraordinary air of charity, gentleness and compassion. That benevolent appearance was of course the effect of his care in not spilling the water and of his attitude as he sat on the sill; for, if a man lingered with his lips glued to the rim of the bucket after Gaspar Ruiz had said 'You have had enough,' there would be no tenderness or mercy in the shove of the foot which would send him groaning and doubled up far into the interior of the prison, where he would knock down two or three others before he fell himself. They came up to him again and again; it looked as if they meant to drink the well dry before going to their death; but the soldiers were so amused by Gaspar Ruiz's systematic proceedings that they carried the water up to the window cheerfully.

"When the adjutant came out after his siesta there was some trouble over this affair, I can assure you. And the worst of it, that the general whom we expected never came to the castle that day."

The guests of General Santierra unanimously expressed their regret that the man of such strength and patience had not been saved.

"He was not saved by my interference," said the General. "The prisoners were led to execution half an hour before sunset. Gaspar Ruiz, contrary to the sergeant's apprehensions, gave no trouble. There was no necessity to get a cavalry man with a lasso in order to subdue him, as if he were a wild bull of the campo. I believe he marched out with his arms free amongst the others who were bound. I did not see. I was not there. I had been put under arrest for interfering with the prisoner's guard. About dusk, sitting dismally in my quarters, I heard three volleys fired, and thought that I should never hear of Gaspar Ruiz again. He fell with the others. But we were to hear of him nevertheless, though the sergeant boasted that, as he lay on his face expiring or dead in the heap of the slain, he had slashed his neck with a sword. He had done this, he said, to make sure of ridding the world of a dangerous traitor.

"I confess to you, senores, that I thought of that strong man with a sort of gratitude, and with some admiration. He had used his strength honourably. There dwelt, then, in his soul no fierceness corresponding to the vigour of his body."

# V

GASPAR RUIZ, who could with ease bend apart the heavy iron bars of the prison, was led out with others to summary execution. "Every bullet has its billet," runs the proverb. All the merit of proverbs consists in the concise and picturesque expression. In the surprise of our minds is found their persuasiveness. In other words, we are struck and convinced by the shock.

What surprises us is the form, not the substance. Proverbs are art— cheap art. As a general rule they are not true; unless indeed they happen to be mere platitudes, as for instance the proverb, "Half a loaf is better than no bread," or "A miss is as good as a mile." Some proverbs are simply imbecile, others are immoral. That one evolved out of the naive heart of the great Russian people, "Man discharges the piece, but God carries the bullet," is piously atrocious, and at bitter variance with the accepted conception of a compassionate God. It would indeed be an inconsistent occupation for the Guardian of the poor, the innocent and the helpless, to carry the bullet, for instance, into the heart of a father.

Gaspar Ruiz was childless, he had no wife, he had never been in love. He had hardly ever spoken to a woman, beyond his mother and the ancient negress of the household, whose wrinkled skin was the colour of cinders, and whose lean body was bent double from age. If some bullets from those muskets fired off at fifteen paces were specifically destined for the heart of Gaspar Ruiz, they all missed their billet. One, however, carried away a small piece of his ear, and another a fragment of flesh from his shoulder.

A red and unclouded sun setting into a purple ocean looked with a fiery stare upon the enormous wall of the Cordilleras, worthy witnesses of his glorious extinction. But it is inconceivable that it should have seen the ant−like men busy with their absurd and insignificant trials of killing and dying for reasons that, apart from being generally childish, were also imperfectly understood. It did light up, however, the backs of the firing party and the faces of the condemned men. Some of them had fallen on their knees, others remained standing, a few averted their heads from the levelled barrels of muskets. Gaspar Ruiz, upright, the burliest of them all, hung his big shock head. The low sun dazzled him a little, and he counted himself a dead man already.

# Gaspar Ruiz

He fell at the first discharge. He fell because he thought he was a dead man. He struck the ground heavily. The jar of the fall surprised him. "I am not dead apparently," he thought to himself, when he heard the execution platoon reloading its arms at the word of command. It was then that the hope of escape dawned upon him for the first time. He remained lying stretched out with rigid limbs under the weight of two bodies collapsed crosswise upon his back.

By the time the soldiers had fired a third volley into the slightly stirring heaps of the slain, the sun had gone out of sight, and almost immediately with the darkening of the ocean dusk fell upon the coasts of the young Republic. Above the gloom of the lowlands the snowy peaks of the Cordillera remained luminous and crimson for a long time. The soldiers before marching back to the fort sat down to smoke.

The sergeant with a naked sword in his hand strolled away by himself along the heap of the dead. He was a humane man, and watched for any stir or twitch of limb in the merciful idea of plunging the point of his blade into any body giving the slightest sign of life. But none of the bodies afforded him an opportunity for the display of this charitable intention. Not a muscle twitched amongst them, not even the powerful muscles of Gaspar Ruiz, who, deluged with the blood of his neighbours and shamming death, strove to appear more lifeless than the others.

He was lying face down. The sergeant recognised him by his stature, and being himself a very small man, looked with envy and contempt at the prostration of so much strength. He had always disliked that particular soldier. Moved by an obscure animosity, he inflicted a long gash across the neck of Gaspar Ruiz, with some vague notion of making sure of that strong man's death, as if a powerful physique were more able to resist the bullets. For the sergeant had no doubt that Gaspar Ruiz had been shot through in many places. Then he passed on, and shortly afterwards marched off with, his men, leaving the bodies to the care of crows and vultures.

Gaspar Ruiz had restrained a cry, though it had seemed to him that his head was cut off at a blow; and when darkness came, shaking off the dead, whose weight had oppressed him, he crawled away over the plain on his hands and knees. After drinking deeply, like a wounded beast, at a shallow stream, he assumed an upright posture, and staggered on light–headed and aimless, as if lost amongst the stars of the clear night. A small house seemed to rise out of the ground before him. He stumbled into the porch and struck at the door with his fist. There was not a gleam of light. Gaspar Ruiz might have thought that the inhabitants had fled from it, as from many others in the neighbourhood, had it not been for the shouts of abuse that answered his thumping. In his feverish and enfeebled state the angry screaming seemed to him part of a hallucination belonging to the weird dreamlike feeling of his unexpected condemnation to death, of the thirst suffered, of the volleys fired at him within fifteen paces, of his head being cut off at a blow. "Open the door!" he cried. "Open in the name of God!"

An infuriated voice from within jeered at him: "Come in, come in. This house belongs to you. All this land belongs to you. Come and take it."

"For the love of God," Gaspar Ruiz murmured.

"Does not all the land belong to you patriots?" the voice on the other side of the door screamed on. "Are you not a patriot?"

Gaspar Ruiz did not know. "I am a wounded man," he said apathetically.

All became still inside. Gaspar Ruiz lost the hope of being admitted, and lay down under the porch just outside the door. He was utterly careless of what was going to happen to him. All his consciousness seemed to be concentrated in his neck, where he felt a severe pain. His indifference as to his fate was genuine.

The day was breaking when he awoke from a feverish doze; the door at which he had knocked in the dark stood wide open now, and a girl, steadying herself with her outspread arms, leaned over the threshold. Lying on his back, he stared up at her. Her face was pale and her eyes were very dark; her hair hung down black as ebony against her white cheeks; her lips were full and red. Beyond her he saw another head with long grey hair, and a thin old face with a pair of anxiously clasped hands under the chin.

# VI

"I KNEW those people by sight," General Santierra would tell his guests at the dining–table. "I mean the people with whom Gaspar Ruiz found shelter. The father was an old Spaniard, a man of property, ruined by the revolution. His estates, his house in town, his money, everything he had in the world had been confiscated by proclamation, for he was a bitter foe of our independence. From a position of great dignity and influence on the Viceroy's Council he became of less importance than his own negro slaves made free by our glorious revolution. He had not even the means to flee the country, as other Spaniards had managed to do. It may be that, wandering ruined and houseless, and burdened with nothing but his life, which was left to him by the clemency of the Provisional Government, he had simply walked under that broken roof of old tiles. It was a lonely spot. There did not seem to be even a dog belonging to the place. But though the roof had holes, as if a cannonball or two had dropped through it, the wooden shutters were thick and tight–closed all the time.

"My way took me frequently along the path in front of that miserable rancho. I rode from the fort to the town almost every evening, to sigh at the window of a lady I was in love with, then. When one is young, you understand . . . . She was a good patriot, you may be sure. Caballeros, credit me or not, political feeling ran so high in those days that I do not believe I could have been fascinated by the charms of a woman of Royalist opinions. . . ."

Murmurs of amused incredulity all round the table interrupted the General; and while they lasted he stroked his white beard gravely.

"Senores," he protested, "a Royalist was a monster to our overwrought feelings. I am telling you this in order not to be suspected of the slightest tenderness towards that old Royalist's daughter. Moreover, as you know, my affections were engaged elsewhere. But I could not help noticing her on rare occasions when with the front door open she stood in the porch.

"You must know that this old Royalist was as crazy as a man can be. His political misfortunes, his total downfall and ruin, had disordered his mind. To show his contempt for what we patriots could do, he affected to laugh at his imprisonment, at the confiscation of his lands, the burning of his houses, and the misery to which he and his womenfolk were reduced. This habit of laughing had grown upon him, so that he would begin to laugh and shout directly he caught sight of any stranger. That was the form of his madness.

"I, of course, disregarded the noise of that madman with that feeling of superiority the success of our cause inspired in us Americans. I suppose I really despised him because he

# Gaspar Ruiz

was an old Castilian, a Spaniard born, and a Royalist. Those were certainly no reasons to scorn a man; but for centuries Spaniards born had shown their contempt of us Americans, men as well descended as themselves, simply because we were what they called colonists. We had been kept in abasement and made to feel our inferiority in social intercourse. And now it was our turn. It was sale for us patriots to display the same sentiments; and I being a young patriot, son of a patriot, despised that old Spaniard, and despising him I naturally disregarded his abuse, though it was annoying to my feelings. Others perhaps would not have been so forbearing.

"He would begin with a great yell—'I see a patriot. Another of them!' long before I came abreast of the house. The tone of his senseless revilings, mingled with bursts of laughter, was sometimes piercingly shrill and sometimes grave. It was all very mad; but I felt it incumbent upon my dignity to check my horse to a walk without even glancing towards the house, as if that man's abusive clamour in the porch were less than the barking of a cur. I rode by, preserving an expression of haughty indifference on my face.

"It was no doubt very dignified; but I should have done better if I had kept my eyes open. A military man in war time should never consider himself off duty; and especially so if the war is a revolutionary war, when the enemy is not at the door, but within your very house. At such times the heat of passionate convictions, passing into hatred, removes the restraints of honour and humanity from many men and of delicacy and fear from some women. These last, when once they throw off the timidity and reserve of their sex, become by the vivacity of their intelligence and the violence of their merciless resentment more dangerous than so many armed giants."

The General's voice rose, but his big hand stroked his white beard twice with an effect of venerable calmness. "Si, senores! Women are ready to rise to the heights of devotion unattainable by us men, or to sink into the depths of abasement which amazes our masculine prejudices. I am speaking now of exceptional women, you understand. . ."

Here one of the guests observed that he had never met a woman yet who was not capable of turning out quite exceptional under circumstances that would engage her feelings strongly. "That sort of superiority in recklessness they have over us," he concluded, "makes of them the more interesting half of mankind."

# Gaspar Ruiz

The General, who bore the interruption with gravity, nodded courteous assent. "Si. Si. Under circumstances. . . . Precisely. They can do an infinite deal of mischief sometimes in quite unexpected ways. For who could have imagined that a young girl, daughter of a ruined Royalist whose life itself was held only by the contempt of his enemies, would have had the power to bring death and devastation upon two flourishing provinces and cause serious anxiety to the leaders of the revolution in the very hour of its success!" He paused to let the wonder of it penetrate our minds.

"Death and devastation," somebody murmured in surprise: "how shocking!"

The old General gave a glance in the direction of the murmur and went on. "Yes. That is, war—calamity. But the means by which she obtained the power to work this havoc on our southern frontier seem to me, who have seen her and spoken to her, still more shocking. That particular thing left on my mind a dreadful amazement which the further experience of life, of more than fifty years, has done nothing to diminish." He looked round as if to make sure of our attention, and, in a changed voice: "I am, as you know, a republican, son of a Liberator," he declared. "My incomparable mother, God rest her soul, was a Frenchwoman, the daughter of an ardent republican. As a boy I fought for liberty; I've always believed in the equality of men; and as to their brotherhood, that, to my mind, is even more certain. Look at the fierce animosity they display in their differences. And what in the world do you know that is more bitterly fierce than brothers' quarrels?"

All absence of cynicism checked an inclination to smile at this view of human brotherhood. On the contrary, there was in the tone the melancholy natural to a man profoundly humane at heart who from duty, from conviction and from necessity, had played his part in scenes of ruthless violence.

The General had seen much of fratricidal strife. "Certainly. There is no doubt of their brotherhood," he insisted. "All men are brothers, and as such know almost too much of each other. But "—and here in the old patriarchal head, white as silver, the black eyes humorously twinkled—"if we are all brothers, all the women are not our sisters."

One of the younger guests was heard murmuring his satisfaction at the fact. But the General continued, with deliberate earnestness: "They are so different! The tale of a king who took a beggar–maid for a partner of his throne may be pretty enough as we men look upon ourselves and upon love. But that a young girl, famous for her haughty beauty and, only a short time before, the admired of all at the balls in the Viceroy's palace, should take by the hand a guasso, a common peasant, is intolerable to our sentiment of women and their love. It is madness. Nevertheless it happened. But it must be said that in her case it was the madness of hate—not of love."

After presenting this excuse in a spirit of chivalrous justice, the General remained silent for a time. "I rode past the house every day almost," he began again, "and this was what was going on within. But how it was going on no mind of man can conceive. Her desperation must have been extreme, and Gaspar Ruiz was a docile fellow. He had been an obedient soldier. His strength was like an enormous stone lying on the ground, ready to be hurled this way that by the hand that picks it up.

"It is clear that he would tell his story to the people who gave him the shelter he needed. And he needed assistance badly. His wound was not dangerous, but his life was forfeited. The old Royalist being wrapped up in his laughing madness, the two women arranged a hiding–place for the wounded man in one of the huts amongst the fruit trees at the back of the house. That hovel, an abundance of clear water while the fever was on him, and some words of pity were all they could give. I suppose he had a share of what food there was. And it would be but little; a handful of roasted corn, perhaps a dish of beans, or a piece of bread with a few figs. To such misery were those proud and once wealthy people reduced."

# VII

GENERAL SANTIERRA was right in his surmise. Such was the exact nature of the assistance which Gaspar Ruiz, peasant son of peasants, received from the Royalist family whose daughter had opened the door—of their miserable refuge to his extreme distress. Her sombre resolution ruled the madness of her father and the trembling bewilderment of her mother.

She had asked the strange man on the door–step, "Who wounded you?"

"The soldiers, senora," Gaspar Ruiz had answered, in a faint voice.

## Gaspar Ruiz

"Patriots?"

"Si."

"What for?"

"Deserter," he gasped, leaning against the wall under the scrutiny of her black eyes. "I was left for dead over there."

She led him through the house out to a small hut of clay and reeds, lost in the long grass of the overgrown orchard. He sank on a heap of maize straw in a corner, and sighed profoundly.

"No one will look for you here," she said, looking down at him. "Nobody comes near us. We too have been left for dead—here."

He stirred uneasily on his heap of dirty straw, and the pain in his neck made him groan deliriously.

"I shall show Estaban some day that I am alive yet," he mumbled.

He accepted her assistance in silence, and the many days of pain went by. Her appearances in the hut brought him relief and became connected with the feverish dreams of angels which visited his couch; for Gaspar Ruiz was instructed in the mysteries of his religion, and had even been taught to read and write a little by the priest of his village. He waited for her with impatience, and saw her pass out of the dark hut and disappear in the brilliant sunshine with poignant regret. He discovered that, while he lay there feeling so very weak, he could, by closing his eyes, evoke her face with considerable distinctness. And this discovered faculty charmed the long solitary hours of his convalescence. Later, when he began to regain his strength, he would creep at dusk from his hut to the house and sit on the step of the garden door.

In one of the rooms the mad father paced to and fro, muttering to himself with short abrupt laughs. In the passage, sitting on a stool, the mother sighed and moaned. The daughter, in rough threadbare clothing, and her white haggard face half hidden by a coarse manta, stood leaning against the lintel of the door. Gaspar Ruiz, with his elbows propped on his knees and his head resting in his hands, talked to the two women in an undertone.

The common misery of destitution would have made a bitter mockery of a marked insistence on social differences. Gaspar Ruiz understood this in his simplicity. From his captivity amongst the Royalists he could give them news of people they knew. He described their appearance; and when he related the story of the battle in which he was recaptured the two women lamented the blow to their cause and the ruin of their secret hopes.

He had no feeling either way. But he felt a great devotion for that young girl. In his desire to appear worthy of her condescension, he boasted a little of his bodily strength. He had nothing else to boast of. Because of that quality his comrades treated him with as great a deference, he explained, as though he had been a sergeant, both in camp and in battle.

"I could always get as many as I wanted to follow me anywhere, senorita. I ought to have been made an officer, because I can read and write."

Behind him the silent old lady fetched a moaning sigh from time to time; the distracted father muttered to himself, pacing the sala; and Gaspar Ruiz would raise his eyes now and then to look at the daughter of these people.

He would look at her with curiosity because she was alive, and also with that feeling of familiarity and awe with which he had contemplated in churches the inanimate and powerful statues of the saints, whose protection is invoked in dangers and difficulties. His difficulty was very great.

He could not remain hiding in an orchard for ever and ever. He knew also very well that before he had gone half a day's journey in any direction, he would be picked up by one of the cavalry patrols scouring the country, and brought into one or another of the camps where the patriot army destined for the liberation of Peru was collected. There he would in the end be recognised as Gaspar Ruiz— the deserter to the Royalists—and no doubt shot very effectually this time. There did not seem any place in the world for the innocent Gaspar Ruiz anywhere. And at this thought his simple soul surrendered itself to gloom and resentment as black as night.

# Gaspar Ruiz

They had made him a soldier forcibly. He did not mind being a soldier. And he had been a good soldier as he had been a good son, because of his docility and his strength. But now there was no use for either. They had taken him from his parents, and he could no longer be a soldier—not a good soldier at any rate. Nobody would listen to his explanations. What injustice it was! What injustice!

And in a mournful murmur he would go over the story of his capture and recapture for the twentieth time. Then, raising his eyes to the silent girl in the doorway, "Si, senorita," he would say with a deep sigh, "injustice has made this poor breath in my body quite worthless to me and to anybody else. And I do not care who robs me of it."

One evening, as he exhaled thus the plaint of his wounded soul, she condescended to say that, if she were a man, she would consider no life worthless which held the possibility of revenge.

She seemed to be speaking to herself. Her voice was low. He drank in the gentle, as if dreamy sound, with a consciousness of peculiar delight, of something warming his breast like a draught of generous wine.

"True, senorita," he said, raising his face up to hers slowly: "there is Estaban, who must be shown that I am not dead after all."

The mutterings of the mad father had ceased long before; the sighing mother had withdrawn somewhere into one of the empty rooms. All was still within as well as without, in the moonlight bright as day on the wild orchard full of inky shadows. Gaspar Ruiz saw the dark eyes of Dona Erminia look down at him.

"Ala! The sergeant," she muttered disdainfully.

"Why! He has wounded me with his sword," he protested, bewildered by the contempt that seemed to shine livid on her pale face.

She crushed him with her glance. The power of her will to be understood was so strong that it kindled in him the intelligence of unexpressed things.

"What else did you expect me to do?" he cried, as if suddenly driven to despair. "Have I the power to do more? Am I a general with an army at my back ?—miserable sinner that I am to be despised by you at last."

# VIII

"SENORES," related the General to his guests, "though my thoughts were of love then, and therefore enchanting, the sight of that house always affected me disagreeably, especially in the moonlight, when its close shutters and its air of lonely neglect appeared sinister. Still I went on using the bridle–path by the ravine, because it was a short cut. The mad Royalist howled and laughed at me every evening to his complete satisfaction; but after a time, as if wearied with my indifference, he ceased to appear in the porch. How they persuaded him to leave off I do not know. However, with Gaspar Ruiz in the house there would have been no difficulty in restraining him by force. It was part of their policy in there to avoid anything which could provoke me. At least, so I suppose.

"Notwithstanding my infatuation with the brightest pair of eyes in Chile, I noticed the absence of the old man after a week or so. A few more days passed. I began to think that perhaps these Royalists had gone away somewhere else. But one evening, as I was hastening towards the city, I saw again somebody in the porch. It was not the madman; it was the girl. She stood holding on to one of the wooden columns, tall and white–faced, her big eyes sunk deep with privation and sorrow. I looked hard at her, and she met my stare with a strange, inquisitive look. Then, as I turned my head after riding past, she seemed to gather courage for the act, and absolutely beckoned me back.

"I obeyed, senores, almost without thinking, so great was my astonishment. It was greater still when I heard what she had to say. She began by thanking me for my forbearance of her father's infirmity, so that I felt ashamed of myself. I had meant to show disdain, not forbearance! Every word must have burnt her lips, but she never departed from a gentle and melancholy dignity which filled me with respect against my will. Senores, we are no match for women. But I could hardly believe my ears when she began her tale. Providence, she concluded, seemed to have preserved the life of that wronged soldier, who now trusted to my honour as a caballero and to my compassion for his sufferings.

"'Wronged man,' I observed coldly. 'Well, I think so too: and you have been harbouring an enemy of your cause.'

"'He was a poor Christian crying for help at our door in the name of God, senor,' she answered simply.

"I began to admire her. 'Where is he now?' I asked stiffly.

"But she would not answer that question. With extreme cunning, and an almost fiendish delicacy, she managed to remind me of my failure in saving the lives of the prisoners in the guard–room, without wounding my pride. She knew, of course, the whole story. Gaspar Ruiz, she said, entreated me to procure for him a safe–conduct from General San Martin himself. He had an important communication to make to the Commander–in–Chief.

"Por Dios, senores, she made me swallow all that, pretending to be only the mouthpiece of that poor man. Overcome by injustice, he expected to find, she said, as much generosity in me as had been shown to him by the Royalist family which had given him a refuge.

"Hal It was well and nobly said to a youngster like me. I thought her great. Alas! she was only implacable.

"In the end I rode away very enthusiastic about the business, without demanding even to see Gaspar Ruiz, who I was confident was in the house.

"But on calm reflection I began to see some difficulties which I had not confidence enough in myself to encounter. It was not easy to approach a commander–in–chief with such a story. I feared failure. At last I thought it better to lay the matter before my general–of–division, Robles, a friend of my family, who had appointed me his aide–de–camp lately.

"He took it out of my hands at once without any ceremony.

"'In the house! of course he is in the house,' he said contemptuously. 'You ought to have gone sword in hand inside and demanded his surrender, instead of chatting with a Royalist girl in the porch. Those people should have been hunted out of that long ago.

# Gaspar Ruiz

Who knows how many spies they have harboured right in the very midst of our camps? A safe—conduct from the Commander—in—Chief! The audacity of the fellow! Ha! ha! Now we shall catch him to—night, and then we shall find out, without any safe—conduct, what he has got to say, that is so very important. Ha! ha! ha!'

"General Robles, peace to his soul, was a short, thick man, with round, staring eyes, fierce and jovial. Seeing my distress he added:

"'Come, come, chico. I promise you his life if he does not resist. And that is not likely. We are not going to break up a good soldier if it can be helped. I tell you what! I am curious to see your strong man. Nothing but a general will do for the picaro—well, he shall have a general to talk to. Ha! ha! I shall go myself to the catching, and you are coming with me, of course.'

"And it was done that same night. Early in the evening the house and the orchard were surrounded quietly. Later on the general and I left a ball we were attending in town and rode out at an easy gallop. At some little distance from the house we pulled up. A mounted orderly held our horses. A low whistle warned the men watching all along the ravine, and we walked up to the porch softly. The barricaded house in the moonlight seemed empty.

"The general knocked at the door. After a time a woman's voice within asked who was there. My chief nudged me hard. I gasped.

"' It is I, Lieutenant Santierra,' I stammered out, as if choked. 'Open the door.'

"It came open slowly. The girl, holding a thin taper in her hand, seeing another man with me, began to back away before us slowly, shading the light with her hand. Her impassive white face looked ghostly. I followed behind General Robles. Her eyes were fixed on mine. I made a gesture of helplessness behind my chief's back, trying at the same time to give a reassuring expression to my face. Neither of us three uttered a sound.

"We found ourselves in a room with bare floor and walls. There was a rough table and a couple of stools in it, nothing else whatever. An old woman with her grey hair hanging loose wrung her hands when we appeared. A peal of loud laughter resounded through the empty house, very amazing and weird. At this the old woman tried to get past us.

## Gaspar Ruiz

"'Nobody to leave the room,' said General Robles to me.

"I swung the door to, heard the latch click, and the laughter became faint in our ears.

"Before another word could be spoken in that room I was amazed by hearing the sound of distant thunder.

"I had carried in with me into the house a vivid impression of a beautiful, clear, moonlight night, without a speck of cloud in the sky. I could not believe my ears. Sent early abroad for my education, I was not familiar with the most dreaded natural phenomenon of my native land. I saw, with inexpressible astonishment, a look of terror in my chief's eyes. Suddenly I felt giddy! The general staggered against me heavily; the girl seemed to reel in the middle of the room, the taper fell out of her hand and the light went out; a shrill cry of Misericordia! from the old woman pierced my ears. In the pitchy darkness I heard the plaster off the walls falling on The floor. It is a mercy there was no ceiling. Holding on to the latch of the door, I heard the grinding of the roof–tiles cease above my head. The shock was over.

"'Out of the house! The door! Fly, Santierra, fly!' howled the general. You know, senores, in our country the bravest are not ashamed of the fear an earthquake strikes into all the senses of man. One never gets used to it.

"Repeated experience only augments the mastery of that nameless terror.

"It was my first earthquake, and I was the calmest of them all. I understood that the crash outside was caused by the porch, with its wooden pillars and tiled roof projection, falling down. The next shock would destroy the house, maybe. That rumble as of thunder was approaching again. The general was rushing round the room, to find the door, perhaps. He made a noise as though he were trying to climb the walls, and I heard him distinctly invoke the names of several saints. 'Out, out, Santierra!' he yelled.

"The girl's voice was the only one I did not hear.

"'General,' I cried, 'I cannot move the door. We must be locked in.'

26

# Gaspar Ruiz

"I did not recognise his voice in the shout of malediction and despair he let out. Senores I know many men in my country, especially in the provinces most subject to earthquakes, who will neither eat, sleep, pray, nor even sit down to cards with closed doors. The danger is not in the loss of time, but in this—that the movement of the walls may prevent a door being opened at all. This was what had happened to us. We were trapped, and we had no help to expect from anybody. There is no man in my country who will go into a house when the earth trembles. There never was—except one: Gaspar Ruiz.

"He had come out of whatever hole he had been hiding in outside, and had clambered over the timbers of the destroyed porch. Above the awful subterranean groan of coming destruction I heard a mighty voice shouting the word 'Erminia!' with the lungs of a giant. An earthquake is a great leveller of distinctions. I collected all my resolution against the terror of the scene. 'She is here,' I shouted back. A roar as of a furious wild beast answered me—while my head swam, my heart sank, and the sweat of anguish streamed like rain off my brow.

"He had the strength to pick up one of the heavy posts of the porch. Holding it under his armpit like a lance, but with both hands, he charged madly the rocking house with the force of a battering−ram, bursting open the door and rushing in, headlong, over our prostrate bodies. I and the general, picking ourselves up, bolted out together, without looking round once till we got across the road. Then, clinging to each other, we beheld the house change suddenly into a heap of formless rubbish behind the back of a man, who staggered towards us bearing the form of a woman clasped in his arms. Her long black hair hung nearly to his feet. He laid her down reverently on the heaving earth, and the moonlight shone on her closed eyes.

"senores, we mounted with difficulty. Our horses, getting up, plunged madly, held by the soldiers who had come running from all sides. Nobody thought of catching Gaspar Ruiz then. The eyes of men and animals shone with wild fear. My general approached Gaspar Ruiz, who stood motionless as a statue above the girl. He let himself be shaken by the shoulder without detaching his eyes from her face.

"'Que guape!' shouted the general in his ear. 'You are the bravest man living. You have saved my life. I am General Robles. Come to my quarters to−morrow, if God gives us the grace to see another day.'

# Gaspar Ruiz

"He never stirred—as if deaf, without feeling, insensible.

"We rode away for the town, full of our relations, of our friends, of whose fate we hardly dared to think. The soldiers ran by the side of our horses. Everything was forgotten in the immensity of the catastrophe overtaking a whole country."

Gaspar Ruiz saw the girl open her eyes. The raising of her eyelids seemed to recall him from a trance. They were alone; the cries of terror and distress from homeless people filled the plains of the coast, remote and immense, coming like a whisper into their loneliness.

She rose swiftly to her feet, darting fearful glances on all sides. "What is it?" she cried out low, and peering into his face. "Where am I?"

He bowed his head sadly, without a word.

" . . . Who are you?"

He knelt down slowly before her, and touched the hem of her coarse black baize skirt. "Your slave," he said.

She caught sight then of the heap of rubbish that had been the house, all misty in the cloud of dust. "Ah!" she cried, pressing her hand to her forehead.

"I carried you out from there," he whispered at her feet.

"And they?" she asked in a great sob.

He rose, and taking her by the arms, led her gently towards the shapeless ruin half overwhelmed by a land−slide. "Come and listen," he said.

The serene moon saw them clambering over that heap of stones, joists and tiles, which was a grave. They pressed their ears to the interstices, listening for the sound of a groan, for a sigh of pain.

At last he said, "They died swiftly. You are alone."

She sat down on a piece of broken timber and put one arm across her face. He waited—then, approaching his lips to her ear, "Let us go," he whispered.

"Never—never from here," she cried out, flinging her arms above her head.

He stooped over her, and her raised arms fell upon his shoulders. He lifted her up, steadied himself and began to walk, looking straight before him.

"What are you doing?" she asked feebly.

"I am escaping from my enemies," he said, never once glancing at his light burden.

"With me?" she sighed helplessly.

"Never without you," he said. "You are my strength."

He pressed her close to him. His face was grave and his footsteps steady. The conflagrations bursting out in the ruins of destroyed villages dotted the plain with red fires; and the sounds of distant lamentations, the cries of "Misericordia! Misericordia!" made a desolate murmur in his ears. He walked on, solemn and collected, as if carrying something holy, fragile and precious.

The earth rocked at times under his feet.

# IX

WITH movements of mechanical care and an air of abstraction old General Santierra lighted a long and thick cigar.

"It was a good many hours before we could send a party back to the ravine," he said to his guests. "We had found one–third of the town laid low, the rest shaken up; and the inhabitants, rich and poor, reduced to the same state of distraction by the universal disaster. The affected cheerfulness of some contrasted with the despair of others. In the general confusion a number of reckless thieves, without fear of God or man, became a danger to those who from the downfall of their homes had managed to save some valuables. Crying 'Misericordia' louder than any at every tremor, and beating their breasts with one hand, these scoundrels robbed the poor victims with the other, not even stopping short of murder.

"General Robles' division was occupied entirely in guarding the destroyed quarters of the town from the depredations of these inhuman monsters. Taken up with my duties of orderly officer, it was only in the morning that I could assure myself of the safety of my own family.

"My mother and my sisters had escaped with their lives from that ball– room, where I had left them early in the evening. I remember those two beautiful young women—God rest their souls—as if I saw them this moment, in the garden of our destroyed house, pale but active, assisting some of our poor neighbours, in their soiled ball–dresses and with the dust of fallen walls on their hair. As to my mother, she had a stoical soul in her frail body. Half–covered by a costly shawl, she was lying on a rustic seat by the side of an ornamental basin whose fountain had ceased to play for ever on that night.

"I had hardly had time to embrace them all with transports of joy, when my chief, coming along, dispatched me to the ravine with a few soldiers, to bring in my strong man, as he called him, and that pale girl.

"But there was no one for us to bring in. A land–slide had covered the ruins of the house; and it was like a large mound of earth with only the ends of some timbers visible here and there—nothing more.

"Thus were the tribulations of the old Royalist couple ended. An enormous and unconsecrated grave had swallowed them up alive, in their unhappy obstinacy against the will of a people to be free. And their daughter was gone.

"That Gaspar Ruiz had carried her off I understood very well. But as the case was not foreseen, I had no instructions to pursue them. And certainly I had no desire to do so. I had grown mistrustful of my interference. It had never been successful, and had not even appeared creditable. He was gone. Well, let him go. And he had carried off the Royalist girl! Nothing better. Vaya con Dios. This was not the time to bother about a deserter who, justly or unjustly, ought to have been dead, and a girl for whom it would have been better to have never been born.

# Gaspar Ruiz

"So I marched my men back to the town.

"After a few days, order having been re—established, all the principal families, including my own, left for Santiago. We had a fine house there. At the same time the division of Robles was moved to new cantonments near the capital. This change suited very well the state of my domestic and amorous feelings.

"One night, rather late, I was called to my chief. I found General Robles in his quarters, at ease, with his uniform off, drinking neat brandy out of a tumbler—as a precaution, he used to say, against the sleeplessness induced by the bites of mosquitoes. He was a good soldier, and he taught me the art and practice of war.

"No doubt God has been merciful to his soul; for his motives were never other than patriotic, if his character was irascible. As to the use of mosquito nets, he considered it effeminate, shameful—unworthy of a soldier.

"I noticed at the first glance that his face, already very red, wore an expression of high good—humour.

"'Aha! senor teniente,' he cried loudly, as I saluted at the door. 'Behold! Your strong man has turned up again.'

"He extended to me a folded letter, which I saw was superscribed 'To the Commander—in—Chief of the Republican Armies.'

"'This,' General Robles went on in his loud voice, 'was thrust by a boy into the hand of a sentry at the Quartel General, while the fellow stood there thinking of his girl, no doubt—for before he could gather his wits together, the boy had disappeared amongst the market people, and he protests he could not recognise him to save his life.'

"My chief told me further that the soldier had given the letter to the sergeant of the guard, and that ultimately it had reached the hands of our generalissimo. His Excellency had deigned to take cognisance of it with his own eyes. After that he had referred the matter in confidence to General Robles.

# Gaspar Ruiz

"The letter, senores, I cannot now recollect textually. I saw the signature of Gaspar Ruiz. He was an audacious fellow. He had snatched a soul for himself out of a cataclysm, remember. And now it was that soul which had dictated the terms of his letter. Its tone was very independent. I remember it struck me at the time as noble—dignified. It was, no doubt, her letter. Now I shudder at the depth of its duplicity. Gaspar Ruiz was made to complain of the injustice of which he had been a victim. He invoked his previous record of fidelity and courage. Having been saved from death by the miraculous interposition of Providence, he could think of nothing but of retrieving his character. This, he wrote, he could not hope to do in the ranks as a discredited soldier still under suspicion. He had the means to give a striking proof of his fidelity. And he ended by proposing to the General–in–Chief a meeting at midnight in the middle of the Plaza before the Moneta. The signal would be to strike fire with flint and steel three times, which was not too conspicuous and yet distinctive enough for recognition.

"San Martin, the great Liberator, loved men of audacity and courage. Besides, he was just and compassionate. I told him as much of the man's story as I knew, and was ordered to accompany him on the appointed night. The signals were duly exchanged. It was midnight, and the whole town was dark and silent. Their two cloaked figures came together in the centre of the vast Plaza, and, keeping discreetly at a distance, I listened for an hour or more to the murmur of their voices. Then the general motioned me to approach; and as I did so I heard San Martin, who was courteous to gentle and simple alike, offer Gaspar Ruiz the hospitality of the headquarters for the night. But the soldier refused, saying that he would not be worthy of that honour till he had done something.

"'You cannot have a common deserter for your guest, Excellency,' he protested with a low laugh, and stepping backwards, merged slowly into the night.

"The Commander–in–Chief observed to me, as we turned away: 'He had somebody with him, our friend Ruiz. I saw two figures for a moment. It was an unobtrusive companion.'

"I too had observed another figure join the vanishing form of Gaspar Ruiz. It had the appearance of a short fellow in a poncho and a big hat. And I wondered stupidly who it could be he had dared take into his confidence. I might have guessed it could be no one but that fatal girl—alas!

# Gaspar Ruiz

"Where he kept her concealed I do not know. He had—it was known afterwards—an uncle, his mother's brother, a small shopkeeper in Santiago. Perhaps it was there that she found a roof and food. Whatever she found, it was poor enough to exasperate her pride and keep up her anger and hate. It is certain she did not accompany him on the feat he undertook to accomplish first of all. It was nothing less than the destruction of a store of war material collected secretly by the Spanish authorities in the south, in a town called Linares. Gaspar Ruiz was entrusted with a small party only, but they proved themselves worthy of San Martin's confidence. The season was not propitious. They had to swim swollen rivers. They seemed, however, to have galloped night and day, outriding the news of their foray, and holding straight for the town, a hundred miles into the enemy's country, till at break of day they rode into it sword in hand, surprising the little garrison. It fled without making a stand, leaving most of its officers in Gaspar Ruiz' hands.

"A great explosion of gunpowder ended the conflagration of the magazines the raiders had set on fire without loss of time. In less than six hours they were riding away at the same mad speed, without the loss of a single man. Good as they were, such an exploit is not performed without a still better leadership.

"I was dining at the headquarters when Gas–par Ruiz himself brought the news of his success. And it was a great blow to the Royalist troops. For a proof he displayed to us the garrison's flag. He took it from under his poncho and flung it on the table. The man was transfigured; there was something exulting and menacing in the expression of his face. He stood behind General San Martin's chair and looked proudly at us all. He had a round blue cap edged with silver braid on his head, and we all could see a large white scar on the nape of his sunburnt neck.

"Somebody asked him what he had done with the captured Spanish officers.

"He shrugged his shoulders scornfully. 'What a question to ask! In a partisan war you do not burden yourself with prisoners. I let them go —and here are their sword–knots.'

"He flung a bunch of them on the table upon the flag. Then General Robles, whom I was attending there, spoke up in his loud, thick voice: 'You did! Then, my brave friend, you do not know yet how a war like ours ought to be conducted. You should have done—this.' And he passed the edge of his hand across his own throat.

# Gaspar Ruiz

"Alas, senores! It was only too true that on both sides this contest, in its nature so heroic, was stained by ferocity. The murmurs that arose at General Robles' words were by no means unanimous in tone. But the generous and brave San Martin praised the humane action, and pointed out to Ruiz a place on his right hand. Then rising with a full glass he proposed a toast: 'Caballeros and comrades–in–arms, let us drink the health of Captain Gaspar Ruiz.' And when we had emptied our glasses: 'I intend,' the Commander–in–Chief continued, 'to entrust him with the guardianship of our southern frontier, while we go afar to liberate our brethren in Peru. He whom the enemy could not stop from striking a blow at his very heart will know how to protect the peaceful populations we leave behind us to pursue our sacred task.' And he embraced the silent Gaspar Ruiz by his side.

"Later on, when we all rose from table, I approached the latest officer of the army with my congratulations. 'And, Captain Ruiz,' I added, 'perhaps you do not mind telling a man who has always believed in the uprightness of your character, what became of Dona Erminia on that night?'

"At this friendly question his aspect changed. He looked at me from under his eyebrows with the heavy, dull glance of a guasso—of a peasant.

"Senor teniente,' he said thickly, and as if very much cast down, 'do not ask me about the senorita, for I prefer not to think about her at all when I am amongst you.'

"He looked, with a frown, all about the room, full of smoking and talking officers. Of course I did not insist.

"These, senores, were the last words I was to hear him utter for a long, long time. The very next day we embarked for our arduous expedition to Peru, and we only heard of Gaspar Ruiz' doings in the midst of battles of our own. He had been appointed military guardian of our southern province. He raised a partida. But his leniency to the conquered foe displeased the Civil Governor, who was a formal, uneasy man, full of suspicions. He forwarded reports against Gaspar Ruiz to the Supreme Government; one of them being that he had married publicly, with great pomp, a woman of Royalist tendencies. Quarrels were sure to arise between these two men of very different character. At last the Civil Governor began to complain of his inactivity, and to hint at treachery, which, he wrote, would be not surprising in a man of such antecedents. Gaspar Ruiz heard of it. His rage flamed up, and the woman ever by his side knew how to feed it with perfidious words. I do not know whether really the Supreme Government ever did—as he complained afterwards—send orders for his arrest. It seems certain that the Civil Governor began to tamper with his officers, and that Gaspar Ruiz discovered the fact.

"One evening, when the Governor was giving a tertullia Gaspar Ruiz, followed by six men he could trust, appeared riding through the town to the door of the Government House, and entered the sala armed, his hat on his head. As the Governor, displeased, advanced to meet him, he seized the wretched man round the body, carried him off from the midst of the appalled guests, as though he were a child, and flung him down the outer steps into the street. An angry hug from Gaspar Ruiz was enough to crush the life out of a giant; but in addition Gaspar Ruiz' horsemen fired their pistols at the body of the Governor as it lay motionless at the bottom of the stairs."

# X

"AFTER this—as he called it—act of justice, Ruiz crossed the Rio Blanco, followed by the greater part of his band, and entrenched himself upon a hill A company of regular troops sent out foolishly against him was surrounded, and destroyed almost to a man. Other expeditions, though better organised, were equally unsuccessful.

"It was during these sanguinary skirmishes that his wife first began to appear on horseback at his right hand. Rendered proud and self-confident by his successes, Ruiz no longer charged at the head of his partida, but presumptuously, like a general directing the movements of an army, he remained in the rear, well mounted and motionless on an eminence, sending out his orders. She was seen repeatedly at his side, and for a long time was mistaken for a man. There was much talk then of a mysterious white-faced chief, to whom the defeats of our troops were ascribed. She rode like an Indian woman, astride, wearing a broad-rimmed man's hat and a dark poncho. Afterwards, in the day of their greatest prosperity, this poncho was embroidered in gold, and she wore then, also, the sword of poor Don Antonio de Leyva. This veteran Chilean officer, having the misfortune to be surrounded with his small force, and running short of ammunition, found his death at the hands of the Arauco Indians, the allies and auxiliaries of Gaspar Ruiz. This was the fatal affair long remembered afterwards as the 'Massacre of the Island.' The sword of the unhappy officer was presented to her by Peneleo, the

Araucanian chief; for these Indians, struck by her aspect, the deathly pallor of her face, which no exposure to the weather seemed to affect, and her calm indifference under fire, looked upon her as a supernatural being, or at least as a witch. By this superstition the prestige and authority of Gaspar Ruiz amongst these ignorant people were greatly augmented. She must have savoured her vengeance to the full on that day when she buckled on the sword of Don Antonio de Leyva. It never left her side, unless she put on her woman's clothes—not that she would or could ever use it, but she loved to feel it beating upon her thigh as a perpetual reminder and symbol of the dishonour to the arms of the Republic. She was insatiable. Moreover, on the path she had led Gaspar Ruiz upon, there is no stopping. Escaped prisoners—and they were not many—used to relate how with a few whispered words she could change the expression of his face and revive his flagging animosity. They told how after every skirmish, after every raid, after every successful action, he would ride up to her and look into her face. Its haughty–calm was never relaxed. Her embrace, senores, must have been as cold as the embrace of a statue. He tried to melt her icy heart in a stream of warm blood. Some English naval officers who visited him at that time noticed the strange character of his infatuation."

At the movement of surprise and curiosity in his audience General Santierra paused for a moment.

"Yes—English naval officers," he repeated. "Ruiz had consented to receive them to arrange for the liberation of some prisoners of your nationality. In the territory upon which he ranged, from sea coast to the Cordillera, there was a bay where the ships of that time, after rounding Gape Horn, used to resort for wood and water. There, decoying the crew on shore, he captured first the whaling brig Hersalia, and afterwards made himself master by surprise of two more ships, one English and one American.

"It was rumoured at the time that he dreamed of setting up a navy of his own. But that, of course, was impossible. Still, manning the brig with part of her own crew, and putting an officer and a good many men of his own on board, he sent her off to the Spanish Governor of the island of Chiloe with a report of his exploits, and a demand for assistance in the war against the rebels. The Governor could not do much for him; but he sent in return two light field–pieces, a letter of compliments, with a colonel's commission in the royal forces, and a great Spanish flag. This standard with much ceremony was hoisted over his house in the heart of the Arauco country. Surely on that day she may have smiled on her guasso husband with a less haughty reserve.

# Gaspar Ruiz

"The senior officer of the English squadron on our coast made representations to our Government as to these captures. But Gaspar Ruiz refused to treat with us. Then an English frigate proceeded to the bay, and her captain, doctor, and two lieutenants travelled inland under a safe conduct. They were well received, and spent three days as guests of the partisan chief. A sort of military, barbaric state was kept up at the residence. It was furnished with the loot of frontier towns. When first admitted to the principal sala, they saw his wife lying down (she was not in good health then), with Gaspar Ruiz sitting at the foot of the couch. His–hat was lying on the floor, and his hands reposed on the hilt of his sword.

"During that first conversation he never removed his big hands from the sword–hilt, except once, to arrange the coverings about her, with gentle, careful touches. They noticed that when ever she spoke he would fix his eyes upon her in a kind of expectant, breathless attention, and seemingly forget the existence of the world and his own existence too. In the course of the farewell banquet, at which she was present reclining on her couch, he burst forth into complaints of the treatment he had received. After General San Martin's departure he had been beset by spies, slandered by civil officials, his services ignored, his liberty and even his life threatened by the Chilian Government. He got up from the table, thundered execrations pacing the room wildly, then sat down on the couch at his wife's feet, his breast heaving, his eyes fixed on the floor. She reclined on her back, her head on the cushions, her eyes nearly closed.

"'And now I am an honoured Spanish officer,' he added in a calm voice.

"The captain of the English frigate then took the opportunity to inform him gently that Lima had fallen, and that by the terms of a convention the Spaniards were withdrawing from the whole continent.

"Gaspar Ruiz raised his head, and without hesitation, speaking with suppressed vehemence, declared, that if not a single Spanish soldier were left in the whole of South America he would persist in carrying on the contest against Chile to the last drop of blood. When he finished that mad tirade his wife's long white hand was raised, and she just caressed his knee with the tips of her fingers for a fraction of a second.

"For the rest of the officers' stay, which did not extend for more than half an hour after the banquet, that ferocious chieftain of a desperate partida overflowed with amiability and kindness. He had been hospitable before, but now it seemed as though he could not do enough for the comfort and safety of his visitors' journey back to their ship.

"Nothing, I have been told, could have presented a greater contrast to his late violence or the habitual taciturn reserve of his manner. Like a man elated beyond measure by an unexpected happiness, he overflowed with good–will, amiability, and attentions. He embraced the officers like brothers, almost with tears in his eyes. The released prisoners were presented each with a piece of gold. At the last moment, suddenly, he declared he could do no less than restore to the masters of the merchant vessels all their private property. This unexpected generosity caused some delay in the departure of the party, and their first march was very short.

"Late in the evening Gaspar Ruiz rode up with an escort, to their camp fires, bringing along with him a mule loaded with cases of wine. He had come, he said, to drink a stirrup cup with his English friends, whom he would never see again. He was mellow and joyous in his temper. He told stories of his own exploits, laughed like a boy, borrowed a guitar from the Englishmen's chief muleteer, and sitting cross–legged on his superfine poncho spread before the glow of the embers, sang a guasso love–song in a tender voice. Then his head dropped on his breast, his hands fell to the ground; the guitar rolled off his knees —and a great hush fell over the camp after the love–song of the implacable partisan who had made so many of our people weep for destroyed homes and for loves cut short.

"Before anybody could make a sound he sprang up from the ground and called for his horse. 'Adios, my friends!' he cried, 'Go with God. I love you. And tell them well in Santiago that between Gaspar Ruiz, colonel of the King of Spain, and the republican carrion–crows of Chile there is war to the last breath—war! war! war!'

"With a great yell of 'War! war! war!' which his escort took up, they rode away, and the sound of hoofs and of voices died out in the distance between the slopes of the hills.

"The two young English officers were convinced that Ruiz was mad. How do you say that ?—tile loose—eh? But the doctor, an observant Scotsman with much shrewdness and philosophy in his character, told me that it was a very curious case of possession. I met him many years afterwards, but he remembered the experience very well. He told me too that in his opinion that woman did not lead Gaspar Ruiz into the practice of sanguinary treachery by direct persuasion, but by the subtle way of awakening and keeping alive in his simple mind a burning sense of an irreparable wrong. Maybe, maybe. But I would say that she poured half of her vengeful soul into the strong clay of that man, as you may pour intoxication, madness, poison into an empty cup.

"If he wanted war he got it in earnest when our victorious army began to return from Peru. Systematic operations were planned against this blot on the honour and prosperity of our hardly–won independence. General Robles commanded, with his well–known ruthless severity. Savage reprisals were exercised on both sides, and no quarter was given in the field. Having won my promotion in the Peru campaign, I was a captain on the staff.

"Gaspar Ruiz found himself hard pressed; at the same time we heard by means of a fugitive priest who had been carried off from his village presbytery, and galloped eighty miles into the hills to perform the christening ceremony, that a daughter was born to them. To celebrate the event, I suppose, Ruiz executed one or two brilliant forays clear away at the rear of our forces, and defeated the detachments sent out to cut off his retreat. General Robles nearly had a stroke of apoplexy from rage. He found another cause of insomnia than the bites of mosquitoes; but against this one, senores, tumblers of raw brandy had no more effect than so much water. He took to railing and storming at me about my strong man. And from our impatience to end this inglorious campaign, I am afraid that we young officers became reckless and apt to take undue risks on service.

"Nevertheless, slowly, inch by inch as it were, our columns were closing upon Gaspar Ruiz, though he had managed to raise all the Araucanian nation of wild Indians against us. Then a year or more later our Government became aware through its agents and spies that he had actually entered into alliance with Carreras, the so–called dictator of the so–called republic of Mendoza, on the other side of the mountains. Whether Gaspar Ruiz had a deep political intention, or whether he wished only to secure a safe retreat for his wife and child while he pursued remorselessly against us his war of surprises and massacres, I cannot tell. The alliance, however, was a fact. Defeated in his attempt to check our advance from the sea, he retreated with his usual swiftness, and preparing for another hard and hazardous tussle began by sending his wife with the little girl across the Pequena range of mountains, on the frontier of Mendoza."

# XI

"Now Carreras, under the guise of politics and liberalism, was a scoundrel of the deepest dye, and the unhappy state of Mendoza was the prey of thieves, robbers, traitors and murderers, who formed his party. He was under a noble exterior a man without heart, pity, honour, or conscience. Tie aspired to nothing but tyranny, and though he would have made use of Gaspar Ruiz for his nefarious designs, yet he soon became aware that to propitiate the Chilian Government would answer his purpose better. I blush to say that he made proposals to our Government to deliver up on certain conditions the wife and child of the man who had trusted to his honour, and that this offer was accepted.

"While on her way to Mendoza over the Pequena pass she was betrayed by her escort of Carreras' men, and given up to the officer in command of a Chilian fort on the upland at the foot of the main Cordillera range. This atrocious transaction might have cost me dear, for as a matter of fact I was a prisoner in Gaspar Ruiz' camp when he received the news. I had been captured during a reconnaissance, my escort of a few troopers being speared by the Indians of his bodyguard. I was saved from the same fate because he recognised my features just in time. No doubt my friends thought I was dead, and I would not have given much for my life at any time. But the strong man treated me very well, because, he said, I had always believed in his innocence and had tried to serve him when he was a victim of injustice.

"'And now,' was his speech to me, 'you shall see that I always speak the truth. You are safe.'

"I did not think I was very safe when I was called up to go to him one night. He paced up and down like a wild beast, exclaiming, 'Betrayed! Betrayed!'

"He walked up to me clenching his fists. 'I could cut your throat.'

"'Will that give your wife back to you?' I said as quietly as I could.

"'And the child!' he yelled out, as if mad. He fell into a chair and laughed in a frightful, boisterous manner. 'Oh, no, you are safe.'

"I assured him that his wife's life was safe too; but I did not say what I was convinced of—that he would never see her again. He wanted war to the death, and the war could only end with his death.

"He gave me a strange, inexplicable look, and sat muttering blankly. 'In their hands. In their hands.'

"I kept as still as a mouse before a cat. Suddenly he jumped up. 'What am I doing here?' he cried; and opening the door, he yelled out orders to saddle and mount. 'What is it?' he stammered, coming up to me. 'The Pequena fort; a fort of palisades! Nothing. I would get her back if she were hidden in the very heart of the mountain.' He amazed me by adding, with an effort: 'I carried her off in my two arms while the earth trembled. And the child at least is mine. She at least is mine!'

"Those were bizarre words; but I had no time for wonder.

"'You shall go with me;' he said violently. 'I may want to parley, and any other messenger from Ruiz, the outlaw, would have his throat cut.'

"This was true enough. Between him and the rest of incensed mankind there could be no communication, according to the customs of honour–able warfare.

"In less than half an hour we were in the saddle, flying wildly through the night. He had only an escort of twenty men at his quarters, but would not wait for more. He sent, however, messengers to Peneleo, the Indian chief then ranging in the foothills, directing him to bring his warriors to the uplands and meet him at the lake called the Eye of Water, near whose shores the frontier fort of Pequena was built.

"We crossed the lowlands with that untired rapidity of movement which had made Gaspar Ruiz' raids so famous. We followed the lower valleys up to their precipitous heads. The ride was not without its dangers. A cornice road on a perpendicular wall of basalt wound itself around a buttressing rock, and at last we emerged from the gloom of a deep gorge upon the upland of Peena.

"It was a plain of green wiry grass and thin flowering bushes; but high above our heads patches of snow hung in the folds and crevices of the great walls of rock. The little lake was as round as a staring eye. The garrison of the fort were just driving in their small herd of cattle when we appeared. Then the great wooden gates swung to, and that four-square enclosure of broad blackened stakes pointed at the top and barely hiding the grass roofs of the huts inside, seemed deserted, empty, without a single soul.

"But when summoned to surrender, by a man who at Gaspar Ruiz' order rode fearlessly forward, those inside answered by a volley which rolled him and his horse over. I heard Ruiz by my side grind his teeth. 'It does not matter,' he said. 'Now you go.'

"Torn and faded as its rags were, the vestiges of my uniform were recognised, and I was allowed to approach within speaking distance; and then I had to wait, because a voice clamouring through a loophole with joy and astonishment would not allow me to place a word. It was the voice of Major Pajol, an old friend. He, like my other comrades, had thought me killed a long time ago.

"'Put spurs to your horse, man!' he yelled, in the greatest excitement; 'we will swing the gate open for you.'

"I let the reins fall out of my hand and shook my head. 'I am on my honour,' I cried.

"'To him!' he shouted, with infinite disgust.'

"'He promises you your life.'

"'Our life is our own. And do you, Santierra, advise us to surrender to that rastrero?'

"'No!' I shouted. 'But he wants his wife and child, and he can cut you off from water.'

"'Then she would be the first to suffer. You may tell him that. Look here—this is all nonsense: we shall dash out and capture you.

"'You shall not catch me alive,' I said firmly.

"'Imbecile!'

"'For God's sake,' I continued hastily, 'do not open the gate.' And I pointed at the multitude of Peneleo's Indians who covered the shores of the lake.

"I had never seen so many of these savages together. Their lances seemed as numerous as stalks of grass. Their hoarse voices made a vast, inarticulate sound like the murmur of the sea.

"My friend Pajol was swearing to himself. 'Well, then—go to the devil!' he shouted, exasperated. But as I swung round he repented, for I heard him say hurriedly, 'Shoot the fool's horse before he gets away.

"He had good marksmen. Two shots rang out, and in the very act of turning my horse staggered, fell and lay still as if struck by lightning. I had my feet out of the stirrups and rolled clear of him; but I did not attempt to rise. Neither dared they rush out to drag me in.

"The masses of Indians had begun to move upon the fort. They rode up in squadrons, trailing their long chusos; then dismounted out of musket-shot, and, throwing off their fur mantles, advanced naked to the attack, stamping their feet and shouting in cadence. A sheet of flame ran three times along the face of the fort without checking their steady march. They crowded right up to the very stakes, flourishing their broad knives. But this palisade was not fastened together with hide lashings in the usual way, but with long iron nails, which they could not cut. Dismayed at the failure of their usual method of forcing an entrance, the heathen, who had marched so steadily against the musketry fire, broke and fled under the volleys of the besieged.

"Directly they had passed me on their advance I got up and rejoined Gaspar Ruiz on a low ridge which jutted out upon the plain. The musketry of his own men had covered the attack, but now at a sign from him a trumpet sounded the 'Cease fire.' Together we looked in silence at the hopeless rout of the savages.

"'It must be a siege, then,' he muttered. And I detected him wringing his hands stealthily.

"But what sort of siege could it be? Without any need for me to repeat my friend Pajol's message, he dared not cut the water off from the besieged. They had plenty of meat. And, indeed, if they had been short, he would have been too anxious to send food into the stockade had he been able. But, as a matter of fact, it was we on the plain who were beginning to feel the pinch of hunger.

"Peneleo, the Indian chief, sat by our fire folded in his ample mantle of guanaco skins. He was an athletic savage, with an enormous square shock head of hair resembling a straw beehive in shape and size, and with grave, surly, much–lined features. In his broken Spanish he repeated, growling like a bad–tempered wild beast, that if an opening ever so small were made in the stockade his men would march in and get the senora—not otherwise.

"Gaspar Ruiz, sitting opposite him, kept his eyes fixed on the fort night and day as it were, in awful silence and immobility. Meantime, by runners from the lowlands that arrived nearly every day, we heard of the defeat of one of his lieutenants in the Maipu valley. Scouts sent afar brought news of a column of infantry advancing through distant passes to the relief of the fort. They were slow, but we could trace their toilful progress up the lower valleys. I wondered why Ruiz did not march to attack and destroy this threatening force, in some wild gorge fit for an ambuscade, in accordance with his genius for guerrilla warfare. But his genius seemed to have abandoned him to his despair.

"It was obvious to me that he could not tear himself away from the sight of the fort. I protest to you, senores, that I was moved almost to pity by the sight of this powerless strong man sitting on the ridge, indifferent to sun, to rain, to cold, to wind; with his hands clasped round his legs and his chin resting on his knees, gazing— gazing—gazing.

"And. the fort he kept his eyes fastened on was as still and silent as himself. The garrison gave no sign of life. They did not even answer the desultory fire directed at the loopholes.

"One night, as I strolled past him, he, without changing his attitude, spoke to me unexpectedly 'I have sent for a gun,' he said. 'I shall have time to get her back and retreat before your Robles manages to crawl up here.'

"He had sent for a gun to the plains.

"It was long in coming, but at last it came. It was a seven–pounder field–gun. Dismounted and lashed crosswise to two long poles, it had been carried up the narrow paths between two mules with ease. His wild cry of exultation at daybreak when he saw the gun escort emerge from the valley rings in my ears now.

"But, senores, I have no words to depict his amazement, his fury, his despair and distraction, when he heard that the animal loaded with the gun–carriage had, during the last night march, somehow or other tumbled down a precipice. He broke into menaces of death and torture against the escort. I kept out of his way all that day, lying behind some bushes, and wondering what he would do now. Retreat was left for him; but he could not retreat.

"I saw below me his artillerist Jorge, an old Spanish soldier, building up a sort of structure with heaped–up saddles. The gun, ready–loaded was lifted on to that, but in the act of firing the whole thing collapsed and the shot flew high above the stockade.

"Nothing more was attempted. One of the ammunition mules had been lost too, and they had no more than six shots to fire; amply enough to batter down the gate, providing the gun was well laid. This was impossible without it being properly mounted. There was no time nor means to construct a carriage. Already every moment I expected to hear Robles' bugle–calls echo amongst the crags.

"Peneleo, wandering about uneasily, draped in his skins, sat down for a moment near me growling his usual tale.

"'Make an entrada—a hole. If make a hole, bueno. If not make a hole, them vamos—we must go away.'

"After sunset I observed with surprise the Indians making preparations as if for another assault. Their lines stood ranged in the shadows mountains. On the plain in front of the fort gate I saw a group of men swaying about in the same place.

"I walked down the ridge disregarded. The moonlight in the clear air of the uplands was as bright as day, but the intense shadows confused my sight, and I could not make out what they were doing. I heard voice Jorge, artillerist, say in a queer, doubtful tone, 'It is loaded, senores.'

"Then another voice in that group pronounced firmly the words, 'Bring the riata here.' It was the voice of Gaspar Ruiz.

"A silence fell, in which the popping shots of the besieged garrison rang out sharply. They too had observed the group. But the distance was too great, and in the spatter of spent musket–balls cutting up the ground, the group opened, closed, swayed, giving me a glimpse of busy stooping figures in its midst. I drew nearer, doubting whether this was a weird vision, a suggestive and insensate dream.

"A strangely stifled voice commanded, 'Haul the hitches tighter.'

"'Si, senor,' several other voices answered in tones of awed alacrity.

"Then the stifled voice said: 'Like this. I must be free to breathe.'

"Then there was a concerned noise of many men together. 'Help him up, hombres. Steady! Under the other arm.'

"That deadened voice, ordered: 'Bueno! Stand away from me, men.'

"I pushed my way through the recoiling circle, and heard once more that same oppressed voice saying earnestly: 'Forget that I am a living man, Jorge. Forget me altogether, and think of what you have to do.'

"'Be without fear, senor. You are nothing to me but a gun carriage, and I shall not waste a shot.'

"I heard the spluttering of a port–fire, and smelt the saltpetre of the match. I saw suddenly before me a nondescript shape on all fours like a beast, but with a man's head drooping below a tubular projection over the nape of the neck, and the gleam of a rounded mass of bronze on its back.

"In front of a silent semicircle of men it squatted alone with Jorge behind it and a trumpeter motionless, his trumpet in his hand, by its side.

"Jorge, bent double, muttered, port–fire in hand: 'An inch to the left, senor. Too much. So. Now, if you let yourself down a little by letting your elbows bend, I will . . .'

## Gaspar Ruiz

"He leaped aside, lowering his port—fire, and a burst of flame darted out of the muzzle of the gun lashed on the man's back.

"Then Gaspar Ruiz lowered himself slowly. 'Good shot?' he asked.

"'Full on, senor.'

"'Then load again.'

"He lay there before me on his breast under the darkly glittering bronze of his monstrous burden, such as no love or strength of man had ever had to bear in the lamentable history of the world. His arms were spread out, and he resembled a prostrate penitent on the moonlit ground.

"Again I saw him raised to his hands and knees, and the men stand away from him, and old Jorge stoop, glancing along the gun.

"'Left a little. Right an inch. Por Dios, senor, stop this trembling. Where is your strength?'

"The old gunner's voice was cracked with emotion. He stepped aside, and quick as lightning brought the spark to the touch—hole.

"'Excellent!' he cried tearfully; but Gaspar Ruiz lay for a long time silent, flattened on the ground.

"'I am tired,' he murmured at last. 'Will another shot do it?'

"'Without doubt,' said Jorge, bending down to his ear.

"'Then—load,' I heard him utter distinctly. 'Trumpeter!'

"'I am here, senor, ready for your word.'

"'Blow a blast at this word that shall be heard from one end of Chile to the other,' he said, in an extraordinarily strong voice. 'And you others stand ready to cut this accursed riata, for then will be the time for me to lead you in your rush. Now raise me up, and, you,

# Gaspar Ruiz

Jorge—be quick with your aim.'

"The rattle of musketry from the fort nearly drowned his voice. The palisade was wreathed in smoke and flame.

"'Exert your force forward against the recoil, mi amo,' said the old gunner shakily. 'Dig your fingers into the ground. So. Now!'

"A cry of exultation escaped him after the shot. The trumpeter raised his trumpet nearly to his lips, and waited. But no word came from the prostrate man. I fell on one knee, and heard all he had to say then.

"'Something broken,' he whispered, lifting his head a little, and turning his eyes towards me in his hopelessly crushed attitude.

"'The gate hangs only by the splinters,' yelled Jorge.

"Gaspar Ruiz tried to speak, but his voice died out in his throat, and I helped to roll the gun off his broken back. He was insensible.

"I kept my lips shut, of course. The signal for the Indians to attack was never given. Instead, the bugle−calls of the relieving force, for which my ears had thirsted so long, burst out, terrifying like the call of the Last Day to our surprised enemies.

"A tornado, senores, a real hurricane of stampeded men, wild horses, mounted Indians, swept over me as I cowered on the ground by the side of Gaspar Ruiz, still stretched out on his face in the shape of a cross. Peneleo, galloping for life, jabbed at me with his long chuso in passing—for the sake of old acquaintance, I suppose. How I escaped the flying lead is more difficult to explain. Venturing to rise on my knees too soon, some soldiers of the 17th Taltal regiment, in their hurry to get at something alive, nearly bayonetted me on the spot. They looked very disappointed too when some officers galloping up drove them away with the flat of their swords.

"It was General Robles with his staff. He wanted badly to make some prisoners. He, too, seemed disappointed for a moment. 'What? Is it you?' he cried. But he dismounted at once to embrace me, for he was an old friend of my family. I pointed to the body at our feet, and said only these two words:

"'Gaspar Ruiz.'

"He threw his arms up in astonishment.

"'Aha! Your strong man! Always to the last with your strong man. No matter. He saved our lives when the earth trembled enough to make the bravest faint with fear. I was frightened out of my wits. But he—no! Que guape! Where's the hero who got the best of him? Ha! ha! ha! What killed him, chico?'

"'His own strength general,' I answered."

# XII

"BUT Gaspar Ruiz breathed yet. I had him carried in his poncho under the shelter of some bushes on the very ridge from which he had been gazing so fixedly at the fort while unseen death was hovering already over his head.

"Our troops had bivouacked round the fort. Towards daybreak I was not surprised to hear that I was designated to command the escort of a prisoner who was to be sent down at once to Santiago. Of course the prisoner was Gaspar Ruiz' wife.

"'I have named you out of regard for your feelings,' General Robles remarked. 'Though the woman really ought to be shot for all the harm she has done to the Republic.'

"And as I made a movement of shocked protest, he continued:

"'Now he is as well as dead, she is of no importance. Nobody will know what to do with her. However, the Government wants her.' He shrugged his shoulders. 'I suppose he must have buried large quantities of his loot in places that she alone knows of.'

"At dawn I saw her coming up the ridge, guarded by two soldiers, and carrying her child on her arm.

# Gaspar Ruiz

"I walked to meet her.

"'Is he living yet?' she asked, confronting me with that white, impassive face he used to look at in an adoring way.

"I bent my head, and led her round a clump of bushes without a word. His eyes were open. He breathed with difficulty, and uttered her name with a great effort.

"'Erminia!'

"She knelt at his head. The little girl, unconscious of him, and with her big eyes, looking about, began to chatter suddenly, in a joyous, thin voice. She pointed a tiny finger at the rosy glow of sunrise behind the black shapes of the peaks. And while that child–talk, incomprehensible and sweet to the ear, lasted, those two, the dying man and the kneeling woman, remained silent, looking into each other's eyes, listening to the frail sound. Then the prattle stopped. The child laid its head against its mother's breast and was still.

"'It was for you,' he began. 'Forgive.' His voice failed him. Presently I heard a mutter, and caught the pitiful words: 'Not strong enough.'

"She looked at him with an extraordinary intensity. He tried to smile, and in a humble tone, 'Forgive me,' he repeated. 'Leaving you. . .'

"She bent down, dry–eyed, and in a steady voice: 'On all the earth I have loved nothing but you, Gaspar,' she said.

"His head made a movement. His eyes revived. 'At last! 'he sighed out. Then, anxiously, 'But is this true . . . is this true?'

"''As true as that there is no mercy and justice in this world,' she answered him passionately. She stooped over his face. He tried to raise his head, but it fell back, and when she kissed his lips he was already dead. His glazed eyes stared at the sky, on which pink clouds floated very high. But I noticed the eyelids of the child, pressed to its mother's breast, droop and close slowly. She had gone to sleep.

# Gaspar Ruiz

"The widow of Gaspar Ruiz, the strong man, allowed me to lead her away without shedding a tear.

"For travelling we had arranged for her a side–saddle very much like a chair, with a board swung beneath to rest her feet on. And the first day she rode without uttering a word, and hardly for one moment turning her eyes away from the little girl, whom she held on her knees. At our first camp I saw her during the night walking about, rocking the child in her arms and gazing down at it by the light of the moon. After we had started on our second day's march she asked me how soon we should come to the first village of the inhabited country.

"I said we should be there about noon.

"'And will there be women there?' she inquired.

"I told her that it was a large village. 'There will be men and women there, senora,' I said, 'whose hearts shall be made glad by the news that all the unrest and war is over now.'

"'Yes, it is all over now,' she repeated. Then, after a time: 'senor officer, what will your Government do with me?'

"'I do not know, senora,' I said. 'They will treat you well, no doubt. We republicans are not savages, and take no vengeance on women.'

"She gave me a look at the word 'republicans' which I imagined full of undying hate. But an hour or so afterwards, as we drew up to let the baggage mules go first along a narrow path skirting a precipice, she looked at me with such a white, troubled face that I felt a great pity for her.

"'Senor officer,' she said, 'I am weak, I tremble. It is an insensate fear.' And indeed her lips did tremble, while she tried to smile glancing at the beginning of the narrow path which was not so dangerous after all. 'I am afraid I shall drop the child. Gaspar saved your life, you remember. . . . Take her from me.'

"I took the child out of her extended arms. 'Shut your eyes, senora, and trust to your mule,' I recommended.

"She did so, and with her pallor and her wasted thin face she looked deathlike. At a turn of the path, where a great crag of purple porphyry closes the view of the lowlands, I saw her open her eyes. I rode just behind her holding the little girl with my right arm. 'The child is all right,' I cried encouragingly.

"'Yes,' she answered faintly; and then, to my intense terror, I saw her stand up on the footrest, staring horribly, and throw herself forward into the chasm on our right.

"I cannot describe to you the sudden and abject fear that came over me at that dreadful sight. It was a dread of the abyss, the dread of the crags which seemed to nod upon me. My head swam. I pressed the child to my side and sat my horse as still as a statue. I was speechless and cold all over. Her mule staggered, sidling close to the rock, and then went on. My horse only pricked up his ears with a slight snort. My heart stood still, and from the depths of the precipice the stones rattling in the bed of the furious stream made me almost insane with their sound.

"Next moment we were round the turn and on a broad and grassy slope. And then I yelled. My men came running back to me in great alarm. It seems that at first I did nothing but shout, 'She has given the child into my hands! She has given the child into my hands!' The escort thought I had gone mad."

General Santierra ceased and got up from the table. "And that is all, senores," he concluded, with a courteous glance at his rising guests.

"But what became of the child, General?" we asked.

"Ah, the child, the child."

He walked to one of the windows opening on his beautiful garden, the refuge of his old days. Its fame was great in the land. Keeping us back with a raised arm, he called out, "Erminia, Erminia!" and waited. Then his cautioning arm dropped, and we crowded to the windows.

From a clump of trees a woman had come upon the broad walk bordered with flowers. We could hear the rustle of her starched petticoats and observed the ample spread of her old-fashioned black silk skirt. She looked up, and seeing all these eyes staring at her,

52

stopped, frowned, smiled, shook her finger at the General, who was laughing boisterously, and drawing the black lace on her head so as to partly conceal her haughty profile, passed out of our sight, walking with stiff dignity.

"You have beheld the guardian angel of the old man—and her to whom you owe all that is seemly and comfortable in my hospitality. Somehow, senores, though the flame of love has been kindled early in my breast, I have never married. And because of that perhaps the sparks of the sacred fire are not yet extinct here." He struck his broad chest. "Still alive, still alive," he said, with serio-comic emphasis. "But I shall not marry now. She is General Santierra's adopted daughter and heiress."

One of our fellow-guests, a young naval officer, described her afterwards as a "short, stout, old girl of forty or thereabouts." We had all noticed that her hair was turning grey, and that she had very fine black eyes.

"And", General Santierra continued, "neither would she ever hear of marrying any one. A real calamity! Good, patient, devoted to the old man. A simple soul. But I would not advise any of you to ask for her hand, for if she took yours into hers it would be only to crush your bones. Ah! she does not jest on that subject. And she is the own daughter of her father, the strong man who perished through his own strength: the strength of his body, of his simplicity—of his love!"

Printed in the United Kingdom
by Lightning Source UK Ltd.
113508UKS00002B/22